The Untamed

Wolf

This is a work of fiction. Names, characters, places, and incidents either are the product of the author's imagination or are used fictitiously. Any resemblance to actual persons, living or dead, events, or locales is entirely coincidental.

For more information, address: olorunsolaadebola@gmail.com

First paperback edition 2022

Book design by Adebola Olorunsola
Illustrated by Olasunkanmi Matelewawon

978-1-80227-448-6 (paperback)
978-1-80227-449-3 (ebook)

The Untamed Adventures of a Wolf Boy

by

Adebola Olorunsola

Key for Arzeth Words

Bobo/Boda – Brother

Ogi – Nigerian cereal

Naira – Nigerian currency

E o Kun Uomo nain – This word that Steve used to greet the SPC means "Hello my children."

Oda – Ok

Olorun – God

Kuli-kuli – Nigerian snack

Jarae – Arzethian slang for "Get on with it."

Baba – Boss

Contents

Part 1

Chapter One

Wolf Boy

Being part-wolf is strange. It is a blessing as much as a curse. The satisfaction of having amazing agility is unmatched, but what use is it when everyone is too afraid to witness it? It gets lonely constantly, and most of my life has been spent with families with no friends.

I live in the southern part of Nigeria, the western part of Africa. A country with different people of various ethnicities and from diverse tribes. The nation is blessed with a vast landmass and rich vegetation. The humidity is usually high at most times of the year. My family lives in a mini-city called Arzeth.

In my language, *Arzeth* means small or forlorn, which strikes me as ironic as it is very much the opposite. My town is one of the strongest in our country as my people were able to protect our territory from foreign invasion. They declared independence from invading British forces, the strongest country at that time. My town's victory makes me proud to be an Arzethian. All thanks to the leadership of our fearless leader—Chief Ojukori.

Chief Ojukori was a great man with a blazing spirit that could burn out any sign of unwillingness or laziness from any of his soldiers. He had portraits all over the Arzethian palace in which he looked stone-faced. Despite this, he was a joyous man with a great sense of humour, no matter how grim his portraits make him seem.

You know, you could call me great as well. I bet you haven't heard of a boy who got over having **three** different sets of parents, being adopted very early within a few days of birth.

My first adoption was unusual as it wasn't by my kind or species. I was adopted by a Canis lupus—also known as a wolf.

Now, wolves were very rare in Nigeria—well, across the whole of Africa, for that matter. With the growing deforestation and human activities, many animal species are now known to go extinct. Africa is close to the equator, so it commonly has hot weather, and wolves do not enjoy the heat. Sometimes I think it was all a dream, but it felt so real. I lived with her for five years, meaning I was six at that time. I learnt the wolf ways, and when I was three, I was practically a young cub.

I was like Tarzan or Mowgli, characters I recently saw in movies.

However, every good thing must come to an end, and my happy life with my adoptive canine mother finished abruptly on a hot day after a shower, I recall.

We were taking a stroll when I heard gunshots in the distance and was completely oblivious of the unfamiliar sound. However, my wolf mother's ears pricked up, and she had her dangerous face on. Then it happened!

She was there one second, and the next… blood was on the wet grass, the silver water was now a terrible red, she was gone…

I can't help but think she was special somehow.

After my mother died, I wandered the forest in search of some sort of comfort and solace.

I was devastated and poured out at least 500 gallons of tears. I was old enough to know what had happened. She had gone permanently, as had my happiness, I thought, until I came across the city one day.

In the jungle, I spent my days in a cave with grapefruits and bananas. I then wandered off, and that's how I found a strange, populated place. I was surprised to see people who looked like me and walked on two legs. This I now know as the city.

On all fours, I trudged along, growling at anyone that stared. And looking back now, I don't blame them. I was naked, after all.

Then I was favoured by God when a family of tourists from Hong Kong passed by.

They seemed nice and were very gentle; they didn't stare in disgust or scoff at me. They just saw me as one of them but less fortunate. The dad was kind, the mum was tranquil, and the son (who was about the same age as me) seemed friendly. Then they adopted me and are now my lovely family.

I swiftly learned the way of humans and was soon a proper, average child.

I remember my first mother vaguely. She was a widow when I was born. She sang a song that always calmed me down when I was wailing like a baby. She had a smile that gleamed on her face as if there was no sadness within. Little did I know, there was…

I now attend school and know a lot of people. We aren't really friends; we just meet in the mall or something and awkwardly say hello. My mum is a friend of their mum, so that's a start. My dad calls me an intelligent boy as I occasionally come home with 85% or more on my tests. Then my brother gets jealous and claims he is good as well, but he only comes home with 60% at most.

He is sometimes annoying, but he is still my best friend. Actually, he's my only friend within my age bracket. His name is Calvin, and he loves games, dim sum, roast pork and Pokémon. He takes after his dad. He also has similar likes to his mum, except that games and Pokémon are replaced with tennis, sumo and classic literature.

I am older than Calvin by three months and more mature by six years. And that is my life so far. Mildly exciting, you might think, but in the past few weeks, it got a lot more exciting...

Chapter Two

Strange Dreams

THE WORLD WAS in peril.

Everything was destined for ruthless extinction. Its only hope was a spectacular boy, a boy with extraordinary superpowers. This boy was me, and I was ready to abolish this catastrophe.

Evildoers beware! DANGER BOY is here!

I looked around to see any villains nearby, but I saw nothing but destruction everywhere. What was the thing that had caused all this? How did I even get here? Since when could I float two feet off the ground? What city was this? These questions buzz around my head.

Dazed, I glanced up to see smoke, thick, black smoke that looked as if it was a smoke beast with huge, golden eyes and a massive overbite. It glided over me, engulfing the sky, clouds and sun. It covered the city in darkness.

Following the trail, I saw the smoke was coming from a company called *Dennis.Inc (Mayor).*

My eyes widened. Dennis had his own company. Not only that, but he was mayor?! He ruled this place?! Oh no.

Dennis is the half-British bully in my school, as his mum is from England. He goes around torturing little kids just for fun with his so-called "friends."

The question was, how was he successful (or fiendish) enough to have his own town? And the mechanism or technology to create the smoke monster which I call "Ojuju": Arzeth for a beast.

I could hear Dennis cackling eerily from somewhere but couldn't see where which was deeply unsettling.

I was about to run away screaming when I saw a big orange beak beside me. I screamed.

"Relax. It's me, Donald Duck," said the beak.

I looked and saw Donald duck himself standing there, impatiently tapping his flippers.

"G-Good morning," I stammer.

"It's the middle of the afternoon," he quacked.

"Oh."

"Anyways, the smoke has destroyed half the population in Toon Land. Bugs Bunny was gone last week. It's also destroying the world: climate change and all that. Never should've elected that Dennis. Little palooka…" Donald muttered.

Then suddenly, the smoke stared at me and said, "Vincent…" in a devastatingly low growl. "Vin… Vin… Vin!"

I woke up with a startle to see Calvin staring at me.

"Wake up!"

He calls me Vin or Vincent because when they first adopted me, I kept on saying Vincent if they called me anything else. This is because I saw it in a comic and liked the name, so he calls me that now. However, my name is Ying, which is the name I agreed they could call me when I was seven.

In case you care to know, here is the variety of names I was called and by who.

- Calvin – Vincent (mostly)
- Mr and Mrs Wong – Ying
- Dennis or any other mean person at school – Wolf-freak or Wolf Boy
- Wolf mum – ruff whoo woof hoo. (Or something like that)

"Didn't your alarm go off?" Calvin asked in his usual American accent that he learned from four years of holidaying in California.

"I don't know," I said, deliberately not looking over at the broken alarm clock.

"Well, you're late for school resumption, and mum is angry," he said as he tossed me my syllabus.

"At least Dennis being the ruler was only a strange dream," I thought, looking on the bright side.

Chapter Three

Dead by 10

My current mother always says a good impression is the best impression. It is the phrase she says every school resumption before kissing us goodbye.

Another thing she said was punctuality is key. This also applies here because if you're punctual, you make a good impression. It shows you're organised, smart and mature. However, getting up early is hard to do when you walk in the park and chase every ball you see because of certain canine instincts you have (and, trust me, there are always a lot of balls in the park).

My mum (the current one) always wants us boys to be the best boys. Above our mates and never average in all things good that we do. This was her top rule, only below 'pray daily.'

So, she wasn't happy to see I had overslept and was running late. Dad was already at work, and Calvin was eating "Ogi" (a traditional custard), which we recently bought from Shoprite (my mum's favourite shop).

I got downstairs, having done all the normal before-school routines: brushing my teeth, showering, etc. But I forgot to wear my trousers and luckily got reminded by Calvin before mum saw and got even more annoyed.

After dressing correctly, I went downstairs again, ignoring Calvin's sniggers, and ate my breakfast of Coco Pops. I then dashed out of the house to avoid any scolding from mum, leaving Calvin behind.

Despite being late, I walked slowly to school, reflecting on my day so far and trying to clear my mind. Doing that, I found out where my dream came from.

Last night, I watched an interview about Greta Thunberg, a social activist, with the President of America. She wants to stop climate change, and I try to help her by pestering my mum about not leaving rubbish or Calvin to reduce the use of electricity. That explains the climate change bit of my dream, but the other things were random, and I have no idea where **they** came from.

Entering the school, I got greeted by Dennis and his gang.

"Fantastic," I say sarcastically to myself. "I just got back, and I'm probably already going to have a bruise".

"Good morning, Dennis," I say, cautiously backing away.

"Long time no see, Wolf-freak," he grins. "Hold him down."

Some of his mates grab my arms firmly. I can smell their putrid breath, and I gag. My face scrunches up.

"What's the matter?" Dennis asks, looking at me curiously.

It might have been my breakfast or something else, but I realise I am going to throw up, so I double over and let it out—right on Dennis' shoes that looked brand new and expensive.

Dennis stares, speechless. "Those… Those were new shoes!" he screamed. "They cost me over 7,000 Naira!"

"Relax, it's only a shoe," I say. It took me a second to realise I said that out loud.

Dennis clenched his fists and approached me. "Let him go," he snarled as he looked more and more menacing with each step.

I gulped.

This was a true test of brain versus brawn.

Everyone on the school grounds was watching. No one ever wanted to miss a fight at Tulips Academy. Almost everyone voted for Dennis because everyone always votes for who wins. Only Calvin and some other kids that were sick of being bullied rooted for me, as well as Aliyah Italongly, the fifth most popular pupil in the school.

I couldn't afford to be embarrassed by Dennis in front of the whole school, except Greg, who was always late.

I was about to make a run for it when a whistle blew, and a bell rang. It was the PE teacher, Coach Gary.

"Is that fighting I see!?" he screamed in his loud raspy voice.

Everyone dispersed.

"That's the bell, people. GO, GO, GO!" he exclaimed

Everyone rushed into the school building.

Dennis went, but not before crossing his finger across his neck, pointing to me, and showing all ten of his fingers. That meant I was dead (hopefully exaggerated) by 10 AM. At least I was spared time by the PE teacher. But come on, I believe in myself.

Philippians 3:14 says I can do all things through Christ that strengthens me. Yes, I can and **will** do this!

Chapter Four

The Fight

THERE ARE SOME things you can't do when you're as small as I was. For example, fight a 6-foot-tall boy with fighting experience and bulging muscles. I ended up in my room, in my bed for two weeks with a black eye, some bruises and a broken spirit. Also, having noted all the things that happened since I woke up and from my origin story, I'm so exhausted!

Well, here's what happened…

I couldn't relax all day. My brain was clouded with questions, and I couldn't think straight. My mind was completely lost in thoughts about the upcoming fight.

The history lesson was next, and I wasn't any less anxious. In fact, I was feeling more anxious, if that's possible. The next time the bell rang, it would be the ring of my doom as it would be 10 AM, which is break time.

I could hide under the slide, maybe. Or just stay inside, but we're only allowed to stay in at break time when we get in trouble or when a teacher has a reasonable reason to watch us instead of enjoying a 10-minute break from the kids, which is understandable.

I tried to develop a plan. What do I have as an advantage? I ask myself.

Let's see; I'm fast, my reflexes have improved over the holidays, I also had the brains. I could evade, outsmart and enforce.

My spirits were lifted when…

"How about you, Mr Wong?" says Mrs Oluwakemi, our history teacher, trying to put on a British accent.

"Heh?" I muttered.

"Not heh, pardon," she said.

She always loved British culture and everything about Britain (I can't say I blame her) and likes to act like a proper Brit. That is why she likes Dennis because he has experienced England before and knows a lot about it. I am surprised she isn't an English teacher.

"Heh?" I say again, confused.

"You say pardon, not heh," she shouts. "And can you answer what is on the board?

"Oh, uh ok, umm…" I glance at the board and don't recognise anything written on there. Mrs Oluwakemi's handwriting is not that legible, which might be why she isn't an English teacher.

I think it says, 'How many countries are in the UK?'

I thought we were supposed to learn about Arzeth and Nigeria's history this year, and this is a bit of geography anyways. Typical Mrs Oluwakemi.

"Four," I reply. "Four states make up the United Kingdom."

"What are you babbling about? That clearly asks where the UK is situated on a map." Mrs Oluwakemi scolded.

Dennis sneered. The others chuckled. I sunk down in my seat.

"Kids, nowadays!" she muttered.

Mrs Oluwakemi would be a great history teacher if she was more tolerant and taught us what we were meant to be learning. And possibly if she didn't get off topic every time. Although, this lightens up the lesson a bit sometimes.

Everyone kept on whispering, and Mrs Oluwakemi got more and more annoyed.

"What's wrong with you children?!" she exclaimed.

Obviously, no one answered.

After an uneventful lesson, it was the time I was dreading for the first time ever; break time!

* * *

At first, nobody noticed the time. I was puzzled: didn't anyone realise it was break time?

Normally someone would point out that…

"Mrs," Femi said.

"Yes, Femi?" Mrs Oluwakemi answered.

"Isn't it break time?"

Everyone stopped the chat and simultaneously looked at the clock. Their eyes grew as wide as my sorrow.

"Oh, so it is. You may all go, I suppose." Mrs Oluwakemi said.

Everyone rushed out of the classroom, screaming and laughing as I slowly trudged my way out the door and managed to evade Dennis on the way out.

When I got out, I headed for the bushy area immediately as I thought I could be camouflaged in there. It turns out I was very wrong.

After about 5 minutes of hiding, I heard footsteps and flinched. He was here; I could hear his breath, along with five other raspy breaths. It looks like he brought the cavalry with him. Nothing sounded promising at that time.

Then, out of nowhere, something grabbed me by my collar. I screamed in fear.

"Aaaaaaaah!!"

I look up to see Dennis' smug face looking back at me with murder in his eyes. He had found me here somehow.

He carried me by my collar all the way to the very centre of the playground, where everyone could see me. I could see what he was doing, and I didn't like it.

He threw me onto the ground, next to an anti-bullying poster that some kids had thrown out.

I was tired from being dragged fifteen feet by my collar, which had choked me profusely.

Dennis cracked his knuckles, and his mates watched out for teachers as everyone else was just watching in awe, even my own brother.

I dodged two punches and a kick, but that was about it. I got beaten up and thrown around like a rag doll for ten minutes straight. I guess I was just a scapegoat for the other kids to show what happens to those who stand up to Dennis.

After this, no one is going to be an upstander, and even if they were, Dennis wouldn't get into trouble as his parents bribe the school every time he gets in trouble. Dennis' reign of terror still goes on…

Chapter Five

Phase One (I)

I MANAGED TO CLEAN the soot and dirt from my face and elbow, leaving only a black eye and a broken spirit. Any existing dedication and po1sitivity evaporated instantly.

While Dennis was beating me, he insulted me, calling me a dirty orphan that doesn't belong with them. That hurt me badly. Although Calvin tried to comfort me, it didn't help much.

What he meant was that the school was the best in this part of Nigeria and was very expensive. Yet Mr and Mrs Wong were very rich thanks to their hard work and dedication. They want me and Calvin to take after them. I'm sure my first mother was hardworking and dedicated as well.

On the subject of my first mother, Dennis' comment got me thinking. I always thought she was… dead, but what if she wasn't? What if… she was still out there?

I have an amazing family now, and we're going on vacation next month to the Caribbean; everything is great… but for how long?

I wanted to know more about my first mother, so I devised a plan. I wanted to venture to the forest where I once lived. I thought I could remember where it was—a few miles from here.

Here were the different steps of my plan:

- Take the local map of Arzeth from Dad's drawer
- Wait till everyone is asleep without dozing of
- Sneak outside of the house precariously
- Go to the forest of which I recently inhabit
- Investigate thoroughly
- Come back at 1 AM, at the latest

It was thrilling. I had never done anything like this, despite my wolf instincts, which I would think would make me more adventurous and daring. However, I'm very cautious. Did I get it from my mother? I would find out that night, hopefully…

It was 4:30 PM. Through my window, I saw the sun descending below the trees, enveloping the town in a scarlet blanket.

Phase one: Steal… I mean, borrow the map from Dad's drawer.

Everyone was downstairs, eating. I had told them I wasn't hungry even though I was mildly starving. This, however, created an opportunity to borrow Dad's map!

I dashed for my parent's room, thinking this was the easiest step of all but then ran into a predicament. In other words…

A WALL!

Since when did Mum and Dad lock their door?

So, I walked downstairs. In the living room, Mum and Dad were sharing a chicken and chips takeaway, watching football: Liverpool vs Chelsea. It was really hyped up, for some reason. They preferred Chelsea and cheered them on.

I voted for the winning team or Wolves (Wolverhampton Wanderers) for obvious reasons, but apparently, most teams are better than Wolves, according to my parents.

"Dad?" I asked.

"Yes?" he answered with a mouth full of chicken.

"I was walking past your room, and I saw it was locked. Why is that?"

"Calvin goes into our room and watches things he's not supposed to on our TV," Mum answered, half listening.

Mum and Dad's TV is the only one with no parental control, so Calvin takes advantage of that.

"Just out of curiosity, where is the key to the lock?"

"A place Calvin will never look," said Dad with a grin but still looking at the game.

"Ok," I said so as not to raise much suspicion.

With that, I left.

"Ok," I thought. "Where would Calvin never look? The fruit bowls?"

I checked… nothing.

At this point, I decided to just forget about the entire plan. It was hopeless anyways.

I went to Calvin's room and didn't bother to knock. He was playing on his computer (unsurprisingly) while eating his takeaway. He was playing *Who's your Daddy?* A game that involved the battle between a baby and his dad.

Who **my** mummy was, I would never know…

"What do you want?" Calvin asked me.

"Just checking on you," I replied.

"If mum sent you here to spy on me-"

"She didn't," I said quickly.

"Good."

I assumed he had homework that he was supposed to do.

We stared at each other for a while.

"What happened to your eye?" he asked. "Oh, it was from the fight. By the way, are you ok?"

"Yes. Just don't tell mum or dad, please."

"Ok," and he went back to his game.

I left the room. I went to the mini-library to forget all my problems by reading about someone else's problem. I picked up *Oliver Twist,* and in its empty space, I saw…

The key!!

Of course! Calvin hates reading like cats hate mice, and like Batman hates the Joker.

Then I picked up the key, ran to Mum and Dad's room, unlocked it, shuffled in Dad's drawer, found the map, and ran out.

Phase one is complete!

Chapter Six

A Few Hours Later...

A FEW HOURS LATER, it was 11 PM. Everyone was asleep, and I hadn't slept a wink! Phase two: complete. Not the easiest by far.

Chapter Seven
The Encounter in the Forest

MY HEART POUNDED in my chest vigorously. I was profusely nervous. This had to work, or else I wouldn't find out about my past. I was desperate to find out.

I gathered various pieces of equipment, a chocolate bar and my courage. I still could hardly believe what I was doing. If I were caught, I would be in big trouble—huge trouble, and all my privileges would go down the drain.

I was burning with excitement, commitment and a bit of guilt. But I had to do this, to satisfy my curious mind that always buzzed with questions I knew I could find no answers to. Until now, of course.

Everyone was sleeping soundly. I could hear snoring, which was fantastic! Phase three is on!

I cautiously made my way down the stairs and into the kitchen.

I looked in the fridge for more snacks as it was a long journey to the forest. I shifted a plate of leftover rice out of the way and saw, right in front of me, a raw chicken. It wasn't cooked or washed. I was surprised, to say the least. I could feel it over my face, the slimy bony bit.

I was shocked, and I'm pretty sure my heart skipped a beat. I tumbled over as I was tiptoeing. Doing this, I hit the plate of rice with my hand, and it smashed on the floor, making a devastating shattering noise, and pieces of plate flew everywhere. I managed to let out only a small shriek, thankfully.

There was silence…

It was over; there was no way no one didn't hear that.

Then I heard footsteps.

I tried to gather as much of the spilt rice as I could then someone came to the kitchen door.

I made a run for it. Out through the back door, I went. And I ran out of the gate of the house.

Phase Three was completed, but at what cost?

It had been 45 minutes, and I was sure I was lost. The map was beginning to look outlandish to me, and as if that wasn't enough, it started raining. I ate a bit of my chocolate bar to get more energy.

Where I was didn't look anything as it did on the map. I was in a forest, though. However, I don't remember it like this.

It had luscious trees with juicy fruits and a sumptuous, cyan river that I constantly drank from. This one just had trees, trees and more thick trees that looked very hostile.

Then I came to the horrific conclusion that… I had the wrong map! This all was for nothing. This map was the map for my dad's hometown in Hong Kong. ☹

So, I crouched there with my hands on my head, soaking wet in my pyjamas.

Suddenly, I heard something rustling in the bushes. I let the curiosity get the better of me, and I approached it. Big mistake!

It leapt at me with gnarled teeth. My advanced agility (not meaning to brag) and reflexes enabled me to dodge it swiftly.

It was a badger, a big, fierce one. What was it doing here, though? It was a honey badger, which was not native here.

This one looked fiercer than the one I saw on TV. This had scarlet, gleaming eyes, devastating green drool and hesitant movements. It kind of looked in pain. Like all this was not of its doing.

It attempted another attack which I dodged. The persistent badger barely broke a sweat and kept on attacking until I tripped and fell down from exhaustion.

It launched one more time, I screamed, and it went quiet… I could hear a very slight sound of the wind, but that was it.

After a while, I opened my eyes to see with great surprise that I was on my bed in my house. I was flabbergasted but too tired to think. With that, I lay back on my bed and fell asleep…

Part 2

Chapter Eight

The Secret Power Club

THE WEEK HAS BEEN undoubtedly one of the more tiring. It was filled with ups and downs, lefts and rights, good and bad.

I was still wondering about the strange encounter I had a few days ago. It seemed distant now, and I am still unsure if it was real or some dream. However, if it was a dream, who caused the mess that Mum was complaining about in the kitchen? I blamed raccoons, which I don't think hang around here, but Mum doesn't know or need to know that.

The person that saw me hasn't spoken up yet. Mum and Dad said they were sleeping like babies because they stayed up late watching the football games that day. This means it was Calvin. He is notorious for going out of his way to look for something bad I did and tell on me. This doesn't happen often, though. So, the one time it does, why not report it immediately? Maybe he's grown up a bit.

All my equipment was returned, so I seemed in the clear. I decide to keep it that way. I was going to go to Calvin and make sure that if he knew about the incident, he kept it a secret.

When I got to Calvin's room, he was surprisingly doing his homework!

"Who are you, and what have you done with my brother?" I exclaimed.

"Ha," he laughed sarcastically. "Mum says I can't use electronics until I finish all homework.

That explains it.

"Ok… did you see anything in the kitchen? Because I can explain…" I said.

"See what?"

"You did see me, didn't you?"

"See what?!"

"Oh, so you didn't see anything?"

"So, it was you!" he gasped, dropping his pen. "You made the mess, and… did other naughty things.

A grin spread across his face, an evil one.

I had just messed up.

"I'm telling!"

"Please don't. I'll do anything," I plead desperately.

Calvin thinks for a moment.

"Let me join your club."

"What club? I don't have a club."

"The power one," he added.

Oh, I better explain.

When we were little, I told him I had a Power Club that all members automatically get superpowers, varying from personality and other things. He actually fell for it—to this day! He thinks my power is intelligence; little does he know, that's thanks to hard work and willingness to learn. I never let him join just to keep the joke going.

"Ok, fine," I try to say as reluctantly as possible. "But you have to take an oath."

"Ok," he said eagerly.

I put my hand on my chest to start, and I make him do the same.

"I solemnly swear not to tell anyone, dead, alive, or a figment of imagination, about the Secret Power Club. I shall be respectful and obey Ying's every comman-"

"Hey, you're just making this up, aren't you?"

"No, I'm not. Continue."

"-and obey Ying's every command. With great power comes great responsibility."

"Good," I said. "Now, slap yourself."

"What?"

"Obey my every command, remember?"

He then promptly slapped himself.

"Great, only testing."

"What about my superpowers?" Calvin asked

"It'll come soon. It takes time."

And guess what? He believed it!

Chapter Nine

A New Club Member

I WAS FOOLISH TO think that after what I did previously, I would be able to forget it. It was on my conscience for a start, which was really bugging me and making me feel guilty. Which I probably deserved.

As if that wasn't enough, I had to go shopping with Mum and Calvin. I do like going out as my hair is longer than the average Nigerian boy, so the wind flows through it. There are open fields where I can run as fast and long as I want, unleashing my inner wolf. Mum doesn't like me comparing myself to an animal, but the similarities in my qualities and theirs are undeniable. You should see my teeth.

Despite the excitement of the outside, I still hate going shopping unless we are shopping for books or encyclopaedias or anything else I enjoy.

And apparently, since Dad isn't here, I can't stay alone because I'm too young.

It has been 45 minutes and 15 seconds precisely—I brought a watch, and I am getting exhausted. We've been standing in the same aisle for so long. Normally it would be another 45 minutes till I'm exhausted, but I'm extra tired from Monday night.

Calvin was trying to test if he could fly now. Kids today, they'll believe just about anything.

He then told me he didn't see anything last night but pretended to. So, I assume he was sleepwalking. I don't know why he told me this, but I'm by no means complaining. That made me feel better.

Then we moved from the shoe section finally but then moved to the clothes section. *Groan*

Another fifteen minutes passed; Calvin was playing on his phone, Mum was still searching through the clothes, and I was staring into space, wondering if we had powers. Then someone tapped me on my shoulder. I looked back and saw a weird alien waving at me with an evil yet goofy grin.

"Arghhh!!" I cry. "Take Calvin, and let me serve you!"

"What?" said the alien in a jokey voice.

"I told you aliens would take over," I told Calvin. "Where are the tinfoil hats? Don't tell me you left them at home!" I was exasperated.

Everyone in the area, plus the alien, started to chuckle, and people took out their phones.

"What?" I asked.

"It's Aliyah, not an actual alien, you duh brain."

"Huh? Really?"

She nodded.

What I didn't see was that it was a costume. And, when I looked, I could see Aliyah's face inside the mouth.

I felt embarrassed.

Aliyah laughed and said she was trying it out for her cousin. They were the same height, and he apparently loves aliens.

Mum and Aliyah's mum was chatting.

After a while, Calvin said, "Hey, we have a secret club; wanna join?"

Then he just told her all about it. Even after the oath!

When he mentioned the powers bit, I went behind him and shook my head to show there were no powers.

She understood. "Well, it's not much of a secret now you've told me, but sure, it seems fun."

"Excellent," I say as if I was never annoyed at Calvin. "First meeting tomorrow at 6 o'clock sharp." Despite the serious tone, I was bursting inside that we had got a new member on the team. At first, I didn't care about the club, but now I think it's going somewhere. We just got the smarts of the squad.

"Ok," Aliyah smiled, and then she and her mum left.

This day just got slightly better.

Chapter Ten

The First Meeting

I HAD PLANNED THE meeting for Sunday afternoon after church. In it, I will tell the squad about my encounter with that elusive badger.

Calvin is taking notes because he has neater handwriting than me, and I couldn't ask a guest to write, could I?

Calvin was feeling equally happy as he thought if his classmates heard he was friends with Aliyah, he would be beyond popular in his class.

It was 6:05 PM, and she hadn't arrived yet. I was starting to think she was only joking, and she didn't want to join our club. Now that I'm thinking about it, it does sound a bit babyish for our age; we were 10- and 11-year-olds.

6:05 turned to 6:15, and Calvin had already given up.

"We could have the meeting without her, I guess," he

suggested, even though our whole church service had been about resilience.

"Yeah, but she's a clever addition, and you're… you," I said, ignoring his questioning look. "We'll give her a few more minutes."

By 6:30, she was obviously not coming. So, we reluctantly began the meeting.

"Ok, the *Secret…*" with this, I glanced over at Calvin, "… Power Club meeting is now in sess-"

Then I heard a knock from downstairs. "Probably Mum's delivery from Dangote," I said to Calvin.

"Boys, Aliyah is here to see you," Mum called out.

Calvin and I stared at each other with shock and trampled each other, trying to get downstairs.

Unsurprisingly, I got there first as Calvin stood on the fifth stair gasping for breath.

"Hi, Aliyah," I said.

"Hello," she grinned.

"Uh… come in," I said

"Sorry for the slight lateness," she said, stepping inside.

"It's fine, better late than never," I reply, even though she was more than slightly late.

Upon seeing Aliyah, Calvin stood up promptly from the fifth stair.

"Let's start," I say.

"The SPC (Secret Power Club) meeting is now in session," I exclaim. "Today's topic, animals!"

I then proceeded to explain my encounter with the badger but not why I set off into the forest. I just told them I felt like it.

Calvin almost knew the full story about what happened that night. Hopefully, he won't report me.

Afterwards, Calvin burst out laughing. "Very funny, Vincent, and do you expect us to believe you?"

"I think we should," Aliyah said." You see, I have experienced a similarly odd encounter just today."

Calvin promptly stopped laughing.

"I saw a… a penguin," she blurted out, looking embarrassed.

"You mean you went to the arctic?" I asked.

"No. Here, near the equator. I know it's hard to believe."

"I knew it!" I said out loud. "I knew something was going on with animals. Calvin, are you noting this down?"

"Oh… uhh… yeah," he said as he began to scribble furiously on his notepad.

While he did that, Aliyah said she wanted to talk to me privately. Calvin spluttered and coughed uncontrollably and rushed to get a cup of water.

"So," she said. "I just wanted you to know that I know

how it feels to be odd, one way or another. I think we can be friends. You see…"

"Hey," Calvin exclaimed, bursting through the room door, amazingly recovered from the coughing. "I'm odd too! I'm not from this country, am I? We can be friends, too!"

"Well, we can be friends as well. We are in the same club, plus Ying and I are different. It's like **really** odd," she said. "You see… I can communicate with animals!"

It went quiet. Calvin stopped complaining.

"It's more like I sense their emotions and translate what they're feeling, and I speak to them through my mind." She explains.

"Wow," Calvin and I say in unison.

"Ok. I say that today's mission is to investigate the animals. Next meeting, we'll talk about our findings."

"Oh," Aliyah said, "I remember something else. That penguin had a dark aura. I couldn't communicate with it; that was also what made me late. I couldn't negotiate with it. Maybe that could help. Calvin, please write that down."

Calvin did as he was told.

"Good," I said. "Meeting adjourned!"

Chapter Eleven

The Black and White Menace Returns...

SCHOOL DAYS PASSED nonchalantly. I was thoroughly looking forward to our second meeting as a club because there's finally someone who understands me.

Sometimes, during particularly boring classes, Aliyah, I, and Calvin casually pass notes to plan for our upcoming adventures.

At one point, I thought I was taking all this a bit too seriously. But possibly saving the world from evil animals (which I assume is what's happening) is definitely something to take seriously.

Saturday finally came after a long week. It was 4:30 PM. I had decided that after we told each other of our findings, we would go on a walk around the neighbourhood to look for any strange animals.

Calvin asked me when he would get his powers, and I told him that with great powers comes great patience.

At precisely 5 PM, Aliyah came into the house with an excited grin. We were all excited.

We got into my room for our second official meeting. "Club kids assemble," I said. This is becoming our new slogan.

"Any news?" I asked.

It was silent. No one had seen anything; that was odd.

"Well, I saw a lion…" Aliyah said.

My face lit up.

"… But it was in a zoo."

My face fell.

"Well, no matter. We're going to explore the neighbourhood for some animals, so let's get started!" I exclaimed.

We decided we would take Dad's old camera, a mobile phone and weapons (or some may say toy guns and swords). Soon enough, we were ready.

After an hour, there was no advance in our investigation. We didn't cover much ground because Calvin had to stop every fifteen minutes to take a break.

"How (huff) about we (huff) go to Steve's farm to (huff) rest?" Calvin puffed.

I was about to scold Calvin when I realised it wasn't a bad idea at all. In fact, it was excellent!

"Calvin, you are a legend!" I exclaimed. "That's a great idea!"

Calvin swelled up with pride and gave the widest smile that he could, which he does when he is proud of himself.

"That's true," Aliyah said thoughtfully, stroking a non-existing beard. "Steve does seem to know everything going on in and out of town. Let's go; what are you all waiting for?" With that, she dashed in front, towards Steve Moochman's large farm.

We got to the farm in no time. Aliyah was ahead, and by the time we got there, she was busy with something... Steve's dog was attacking her!

We were shocked—stuck to the spot.

"A little help, please!" Aliyah exclaimed

We rushed to help her and pulled the dog off her. It was Bingo. Steve's once-loyal but now fierce terrier.

It was about to launch at us when a hairy, bulky hand grabbed hold of it.

"Down, boy!" A gruff voice said.

In front of us was a jolly-looking middle-aged man. It was Steve! The owner of this farm.

He placed a collar on Bingo's neck that gave him a series of tiny static shocks, calming him down, and he fell asleep.

"E O Kun Omo nain," he said, smiling at us. "Sorry, I don't know what got into him. He's been acting like this since yesterday, so I got this collar from my carrot sales money to calm him down and keep my arm!" With that, he burst into a hearty laugh.

We laughed back awkwardly.

"Steve, we just want to ask you a few questions, if that is alright?" I asked.

"Oda, oda," he replied.

"Great," I say. "Calvin, take notes."

Calvin brought out a scrunched-up piece of paper from his trousers to write on. "I'll stick it in my pad later," he said.

"So, we are investigating the animals around the area as they've been acting strange or found where they're not supposed to be, like penguins found here or honey badgers which aren't found in this town because of its extremely hot weather."

"I see," said Steve thoughtfully.

"So, have you seen anything strange by any chance?"

"As a matter of fact, I did. The other day I saw something with black spots on their eyes and like bears, but lazier?"

"Pandas," I said.

"Mm-hm. Pandas. I nearly lost my finger, thanks to them. Didn't know the little critters were that fierce."

"They aren't," Aliyah said. "At least, not as much as what you just said."

"I don't know what the world is coming to, "Olorun, I protect me too." With that, Steve coughed from saying "oo" too much.

Suddenly, I felt a tingling sensation in me. "Aliyah, Calvin, duck!" I shout and push them down as they narrowly avoid the familiar black and white blur that shot from the grove of maize.

It was the black and white menace. The same badger I saw that day in the forest.

"Back, foul beast! I rebuke you in the name of Jesus, in the name of Jesus, in the name of..."

Then it lunged at Steve with gnarled fangs, knocking him off his feet and into his maize plants.

"Steve!" Calvin shouted.

The badger turned its attention to us. It approached us slowly, growling and building a killer suspense as our guards were up high.

It was just about to lunge; I performed my defence position, Aliyah did her attack position and Calvin, his retreat position. Then as its feet lifted from the ground, it was instantly electrocuted. It let out a yowl and promptly fell to the ground, steaming and unconscious.

And behind it was none other than Steve, our hero, holding a taser labelled *Pest Control.*

Steve grinned, Calvin fainted, and Aliyah and I cheered.

Steve went into his cottage behind his farm briefly and came back holding some kind of cylinder with buttons and a manual.

"Store the critter in here, and here's a manual for it," he said, handing it over.

"Thank you so much, Steve," Aliyah said. "How could we ever repay you?"

"God will repay me. Amen," he replied, smiling and looking at the sky.

Calvin woke up.

"Come on, let's go, Calvin," I say. With that, we walked off into the sunset, carrying our step closer to success.

Chapter Twelve

The SPC's Done it Again

THE SPC (SECRET POWER CLUB) was in Calvin's video game-infested room. Posters of games, magazines of games, game systems, fan art, and lots more were everywhere. We agreed to use Calvin's room during the work, and he seemed very eager. He probably wants to show off his good, expensive things to a visitor.

We were in a predicament because none of us were brave enough to lay a finger on the badger. I was pretty much a half carnivore, considering my fangs and instincts, so I had a handful of experience with them. We all liked and appreciated our arms and preferred to keep them till we were 90.

Mum couldn't help us because the club was secret; besides, she wouldn't be willing to have an animal in our household. We stood, staring at the cylinder container with the badger in.

Suddenly, the door opened slightly. The good thing about Calvin's room is that the door is very draggy. If you don't want anyone to get in your room or see something you don't want them to see, it's very useful.

We hurriedly hid our experiment and grabbed some random comics to pretend that's what we were doing: innocent kids engaging in a reading club.

After a drag, the door flung open to show Mum, red in the face from pushing, with one of her hands holding three packets of *Kuli-kuli*—a popular snack made from groundnut.

"Anyone want some "kuli-kuli"?" Mum asked.

Before Calvin could say yes, I said in my most polite voice, "No, thank you very much, Mother. We're engrossed with our book and don't want to be distracted." I glanced at Calvin to signal him to stop his drooling.

"Oh, ok," she said. "Maybe later?"

"That'd be great," I said, smiling, my tiny fangs glitter in the light.

"Oh, Papa Ajasco is on, Mum," Calvin added.

"Sweet cheese!" Mum exclaimed and rushed out of the room.

We all laughed.

A few minutes after we brought the experiment, the door jolted open so fast that we couldn't react.

Steve appeared before us. The SPC had just got a lot less secret.

"*Ekasun*. I thought you might need a little bit of help."

"Do we ever," Calvin said. And then proceeded to blab everything about our entire club—again! After he finished, he asked if Steve had brought something to eat, which he had.

"Here you go," Steve said, lobbing a cob of corn at Calvin.

"Yeah!" Calvin exclaimed.

"So could you help, please? You **were** once a vet," Aliyah said.

"Assistant vet, but yes, I have a bit of experience with critters," Steve said.

"I'll take notes," I said.

"Be my guest," Calvin said with his mouth full.

I took Calvin's notepad and flipped through video game tips and doodles to get to a blank page and wrote in big letters:

BADGER EXAMINATION

Steve took it out of the cylinder container and examined its teeth.

"It looks a bit like yours, Ying, doesn't it?" He said, laughing.

"I guess," I mutter as I note it down.

"Very strong jaws as well," Steve said.

"Very… strong… jaws," I mutter as I write everything thoroughly. "Check its bone and muscles."

"They're nice and healthy," he replies, and I proceed to write down.

"I'll try to access its memories, thoughts and aura," Aliyah says.

She is silent for a few seconds.

"I can't do it; a strong, negative force is blocking it. I can't get into his mind; it's like a firewall."

Steve feels its heart. "It's fast, a bit too fast, actually." Steve sounds concerned.

Calvin then interrupts. "Guys, I've found something on its neck!"

We look and see a collar. Surely this wasn't someone's pet.

On it was a "V" written in vindictive art style. The art style was a bit like the one I saw in my dream! Maybe my dream wasn't only a dream but also a vision.

Steve removed the collar, and, upon doing that, the badger woke up with a start. But instead of attacking ferociously, it hissed. It had normal black eyes instead of bright red. It looked relieved of the pain of some sort.

It ran out of Steve's lap and out the window after staring back at us as if telling us something.

"It said thank you" Aliyah smiled. "The negative aura is gone. It's free. It seems the collar was sort of hypnotizing it…"

"We shall all be free in the mighty name of Jesus," Steve says.

"Amen," we all said.

"So, I assume Steve is a member of the club," I said.

"Oh no, I have other things to work towards. I think I want to be a vet and a farmer now," Steve said.

"Congrats!" I said. "Good luck!"

"Bless y'all. Bye."

With that, he left.

"Next meeting on Saturday?" Aliyah suggested.

"Agreed," I said. "Meeting adjourned."

Part 3

The Excitement Intensifies

Chapter Thirteen

Operation Lone Wolf

I COULDN'T SLEEP A WINK the following night. I was too excited about… everything! The SPC had just figured out what was wrong with the animals and was going to solve it soon. Soon was too long, though; I wanted to do it straight away. But of course, our school studies and everyday curriculum prevent us from doing it right then.

I was staring blankly at my ceiling, thinking about the club and schoolwork (that was important too). I wanted to look at something else other than my dark room, so I opened the curtains, which turned out to be a big mistake.

My hair stood on end, and I threw my head back and let out a loud howl. I couldn't control it. It was an instinct.

Unsurprisingly, Mum and Dad came rushing into the room.

"What happened? Where are they?! Where are those raccoons?" Dad exclaimed, swinging his baseball bat in the air frantically.

"Everything is alright, Chan; it's just Ying again. Ying, what did I tell you about being exposed to the full moon?" Mum said.

"I didn't know it was a full moon," I protested.

"Just… please go to sleep," said Mum, tired and leading Dad to their room.

I tried to go to sleep but couldn't. Thoughts were buzzing around my head like fireflies. This club was making progress… but what if it isn't enough? What if… we are too late by Saturday?

I glanced at the collar on my side lamp table—the one we took from the honey badger's neck. I took it, examined it intently and accidentally found a tiny button. I tapped it, and the central bit opened, showing a map. It displayed where I was and a "V" mark somewhere around the southwest from here. I immediately assumed this was how the animals knew where to go—by some amazing technology!

This meant another lone wolf night mission!

I would follow the GPS thing to where the V was and thwart it along with its plan and become a hero. Then my mission would be complete.

Starting now, Operation Lone Wolf is a go!

Chapter Fourteen

The Company

PRAISING MYSELF FOR my ingenious plan, I leapt out of bed, ready for my upcoming adventure.

I wrote a note and placed it on my bed in case the worst happened. I also packed a torch and my spy kit that included binoculars, sleek, leathery clothing, a zip line launcher, and a mobile watch. It was one of my cooler birthday gifts from when I was little.

Cautiously, I slipped out through the backyard door (that Mum had forgotten to lock again) and into the garage to get my transport vehicle.

Passing the abandoned boxes and bags, I went to the end of the garage, filled partially with cobwebs, where there was the latest version of the *Ride It All* bicycle: the most popular bicycle brand all over the internet right now.

I silently got on it and rode away. My hair blew in the wind and across my face. The streets were quiet and empty, which was strange.

I was trained on how to ride a bike one-handed, which proved helpful now. I needed to hold the collar and follow its map to the big source of all this, as well as ride my bike.

I was getting exceedingly worried as the compass was leading me very far from home, and I wasn't sure I could memorise the way back. The previously serene silence was now eerie.

The lights seemed to flicker, and a flurry of bats flew past me, scaring me into oblivion. "Stupid, no-good bats," I muttered.

I always hated bats. No, that's an understatement. I strongly detest bats. I don't like rodents that aren't hamsters. Calvin's cousin, Michelle, visited once, and she had a pet hamster that I grew quite attached to if it didn't defecate (poo) while I was holding it.

I thought of turning back, but thanks to fierce determination (or stupidity), I decided to continue...

After ten minutes of following the compass, I finally got closer to my checkpoint. Closer and closer until...

BAM!

I slammed myself into a wall.

Everything went blurry. It took me a while to clear my vision, and when I did, I saw my bike's bell had fallen off. This was unfortunate. It was the best part, only second to its speed.

Then I realised I had spent so long looking, and all I had come across was this wall. I double-checked; I was definitely where I was supposed to be.

ARGHHHHH!!!

Out of frustration, I threw the collar at the wall, trying to break it, but then the wall spoke: "*Collar identified.*" The wall opened into a waterfall, then a vault, then there was a titanium wall that opened into a marvellous sight.

A company, **the** company! A gargantuan beauty.

"I, Ying Chinchow, am fantastic!" I beamed.

Chapter Fifteen

Operation Infiltration

I HAD NEVER SEEN A building as large as this. It had magnificent foundations building up with multiple layers of majestic buildings. There was a vague humming coming from the top floor that could barely be seen. It was painted in dark violet and forest green. In the middle was the "V," similar to the one on the collar.

The company was a breathtaking sight indeed. In the distance, beyond the meadow, were guards. Thankfully, they were asleep; but for how long? I didn't want to stay here to find out.

I parked my bike and took a deep breath. This was clearly the source of all the shenanigans going on around town. This looked harder than I thought. No, I shall remain undeterred and resolute.

I took one step out of under the tree and… "Awooooooh!" I howled. *Oh no.*

"Ugh?" groaned one of the guards, a short, grumpy-looking man. "Tegwalo wake up, Tegwalo! It's your shift, Dundee."

"Er?" aid the other one groggily, a tall, lazy-looking man. "What do you want, Benedict?"

"What I want is for you to do your shift, Jarae."

"Eh?"

"Are you deaf, you…?" Benedict stops as he sees me in front of him. "Intruder! What are you doing here?!" He screams and stands up from his chair.

Tegwalo stands up, and I am terrified. He is freakishly tall and looks like a skeleton from my nightmares. They were opposites. Benedict is very short and takes his job seriously, while Tegwalo is really tall and doesn't.

"It doesn't matter," Benedict says and then pulls out a gun! "You won't make it out of here!"

"Tegwalo! Laser gun, now!" Benedict exclaims.

"'Kay Bobo," he replies and does the same.

I'm shocked for some reason—or it could be that I've never been confronted before.

Benedict makes a move and shoots.

I avoid it narrowly and move backwards precariously.

He does it again, and I duck behind a bush. I know he is going to shoot aimlessly at the bush and might hit me, so I retaliate with a leap from behind the bush and a swift karate kick to Benedict's face. I use him as a jump pad and backflip, landing and performing a victory howl.

"Awoooooh," I scream at the moon.

Tegwalo finally wakes up. "Eh? Oh, intruder!" and he tries to blast me again, but I skilfully dodge.

I get into a vibe. "Is that all you've got?" And with that, I deliver a swift blow to Tegwalo's stomach and a hard kick between his legs.

He shrieks and falls to the ground.

Then, out of nowhere, I get grabbed by Benedict from behind and bonded.

"Not so fast," I say and break free, running with incredible speed all around the building twice. This leaves Benedict dazed so I can grab him by his arm and lob him across the field.

I let out a massive howl.

"Awoooooooooooooooooooooooooooooooohhhh-hhhhhhhhhhh! Operation infiltration is in session," I say, grinning.

Chapter Sixteen

Captured

I AM FEELING QUITE confident after I defeated two fully grown men by myself. Not every eleven-year-old can do that, yet I did it without breaking a sweat. So surely, I could take down a whole organisation with a scrape being the worst injury.

I "borrowed" Tegwalo and Benedict's laser guns for some utility, as well as Benedict's key card to enter the building.

The stealthy approach was best for this mission. I assumed I could not take out over a thousand well-trained men/women, even though I could take down one man (Tegwalo doesn't count, as he wasn't even trying).

Benedict's uniform was the closest to my size, so I put it on to disguise myself. Then I noticed how sweaty Benedict was. It was very uncomfortable, and the smell was deeply unbearable.

I suddenly felt faint and realised I was holding my breath. Alarmed, I took a huge gasp of air, but that only made it worse. I shook it off eventually and went in.

It was gigantic! It was bigger on the inside than the outside and had an even larger collection of people and stairs.

Going in, the first thing I noticed was the wonderful yet queer aroma floating nonchalantly across the vast corridors.

Everyone was wearing the same uniform I was wearing: a jet-black jumper with a bow tie and a V in the middle. I still need to figure out what the "V" stands for.

I stood out as I was the only child there, but no one seemed to notice, thankfully.

"Amazing." I breathed in awe at the magnificent building.

The walls were silver, and you couldn't see the roof for miles.

I looked around and spotted an elevator for those who dislike using the stairs, and beside it was a map. Just what I needed!

I rushed to it, but before I could get it, a man blocked my way. I curtly brought out my laser guns and aimed at him. However, due to my reflexes, he brought his out almost twice as fast and shot, barely missing me. I yelled out and took a look at the burning spot on the wall.

I dropped my guns and put my hands in the air. He cautiously put his guns in his pockets.

He was a burly man with one of those perfect body structures. He was like a more buffed, younger version of Steve.

"Who are you? I haven't seen you around here before," he asked suspiciously.

"Oh, I'm..." I said, playing for time. I looked at a mop leaning on a wall. "... Mop..." I also spotted some apple juice on a table. "... Appleton. Yes, Mop Appleton. That's me," I said nervously.

"Mm-hm. You're a bit young to be here," he said.

I tried my best to look offended. "Are you making fun of my condition!?" I scolded in annoyance.

"Oh, so sorry. Uh... I am George Abelson. Vice president and leader of bodyguards in Vector enterprises. We'll crush the world with our animal army, eh Mop Appleton?" he said, grinning.

"Who's Mop Appleton?" I asked, puzzled.

"You are," he said.

"Oh, sorry. I suffer from short-term memory loss" I lied again.

"Poor you, and remember, stay vigilant. There's an impostor among us." With that, he walked away.

I barely stopped myself from laughing and grabbed the map. I then perused it.

"George Able-something. I need your assistance," I called out.

He turns around. "Yes?" he said.

"Where is the head of the company? I have an appointment with him."

He seemed puzzled.

"Oh, ok," he said, and he pointed to where the head of the company's office was on the map.

"Thank you!" I shouted as I ran up the stairs.

"This should be it," I said as I stood in front of the door: the door to the creator of this madness. I breathed and opened the door.

There is an empty room the size of a ballroom. No furniture, no pictures, no decoration, no anything! "I must have taken a wrong turn somewhere," I said to myself.

"Oh, but you are in the right place," said an all too familiar voice behind me.

I turn to see George. "George? What are you doing here?" I asked.

"You'll find out soon enough, intruder."

Then out of nowhere, guards appear carrying electric pokers.

"You thought I fell for it, didn't you?" George grinned. "Did anyone ever tell you you're a terrible actor? And Mop Appleton? What a ridiculous name!"

The guards approached me menacingly from all directions.

I tried to shoot them with my laser gun, but they evaded it easily. They were obviously better trained than Benedict and Tegwalo.

I bared my fangs at them.

"Fascinating," George said, marvelling at my wolf-like teeth. "The baba will like that! Get him, boys!"

With that, I blacked out and felt myself being dragged. I had been well and truly captured.

Chapter Seventeen

Vector "The Baba"

I GROGGILY OPENED MY weary eyes, and I blinked repeatedly to understand what I was seeing.

The room was difficult to describe but easy to admire. Let me put it as simply as I can. Imagine your bedroom, and if you do not have one, imagine a room in your house. Then picture it about the same size as two large garages joined together. Then imagine it with lots of computers and technology. That is what I was witnessing right then.

Every computer in the room was turned on, and there was this really big one, the size of a bed, that stood out a lot.

Someone was using this computer and tapping on its huge keyboard. This person was silhouetted by the moon, so I could tell it was male. He looked burly and had great hair. I soon realised it was George, the scoundrel. He was part of this horrible organisation that mistreats poor animals.

It was at that moment I realised I was in mid-air. My hands and legs were cuffed with some kind of blue metallic ball.

I took a closer look and saw it was one of those electric spherical things that trap arms and legs. I had seen them in spy movies and even non-spy movies. It was another "easy to admire but hard to describe" thing.

"George!" I exclaimed.

He looked at me. "Oh, you're finally awake."

"Yes, I am, and you will release me at once!" I growled.

"No need to be so fierce," he taunted. "I'll just press this button..." he indicated to a big black button by a bronze whale statue. "... and set you free..."

I wasn't convinced.

"... or not," he laughed.

"I advise you do not taunt the prisoner," said a voice behind me.

"Rx-100," muttered George.

I turned my head to see a tiny green and purple robot floating feebly.

"I am programmed to give followers of baba Vector advice and assistance," says Rx-100. "I shall not deprive myself of my job."

Rx-100 was a tiny robot and didn't seem threatening in the least. It had a screen where its face was meant to be that projected its emotions.

"I'll deprive you of your body if you don't shush," George snarled.

"Should I report your behaviour to baba Vector? He would hate his most trusted advisor to be tormented by a worker."

"Don't... please," George pleaded through gritted teeth.

I got bored, so I decided to start a conversation with Rx-100.

"So, what does Rx-100 stand for?" I asked him.

"Respectful Xenon," he replied.

"Isn't Xenon a kind of gas?" I asked.

"Why yes, I happen to be made from this due to Vector's amazing mind."

"Why was George so afraid of you telling vector, your boss?"

"I am Vector's closest ally. Anyone that bothers me will be terminated. ☺ You may be next," Rx-100 added.

"I thought **George** was his closest," I said.

"Really? Is that what he told you?" Rx-100 laughed, staring at George.

"Done!" George exclaimed. "The ray is set. This next one will round up half the animal population on earth."

"Good work, Gorge," said Rx-100.

"It's George," he corrected.

"Whatev… EV… ever," Rx-100 said with a mischievous grin projecting on its screen.

"The boss is late," George said. "I'll go get him."

Rx-100 and I waited, speechless and in awkward silence.

After a while, George burst through the door.

"Here comes the one, the only, Vector!!!!" he screamed.

I laughed timidly as I saw a figure emerge from the door. It was a dog. "More like Vec-dog!" I said, laughing.

"Shoo, Brux," said George as he shooed the dog away.

Ahem "Here is… Lord Vector!!!!" he screamed again.

And then, the unhealthiest-looking man I have ever seen came through the door. He seemed to have been glued to his chair, and he was carrying a jumbo packet of Cheese Balls.

I chuckled again.

"Jason, the medical centre is that way," George said, pointing two doors from here.

He tries again. "Here comes the one, the only, Lord Vector!!!!"

Then a shady, villainous man came in, pushing George away and approaching me, his cape dragged across the ground.

"Hello, intruder," he said in a voice that sounded like nails on a chalkboard. I looked down at him, trying to be menacing.

Vector had arrived! I shuddered.

Chapter Eighteen

A Truly Vile and Wicked Man

VECTOR AND I EXCHANGED chilling stares; both of us were silent and hostile. This was the vile man behind it all: Vector.

Vector was a tall, sinewy man dressed in all black. He had bags under his eyes and a malevolent grin on his pale face.

I then regretted coming here alone. Looking back, it was a very foolish idea, and I had failed my clan miserably. I didn't let it get to me, though. I couldn't show signs of weakness.

I spoke up. "I am Ying Chinchou, president of..." I trailed off. He couldn't know the actual name; it was ridiculous. "... A top-secret organisation for highly professional spies," I finished, even though this wasn't exactly true.

"I see," he said. "And I assume your crew is… somewhere else. Surely you didn't come alone?" he grinned.

"Uh… no, of course not!" I exclaimed.

"Hmm… your crew are taking their time in rescuing their oh-so-strong leader," he said, smiling fiendishly.

"Their time, place and manner is my business, not yours," I told him fiercely.

His smile faded. "Shock him," he said coldly.

With that, I felt a small tingle in my fingers first, and then my whole body got electrocuted with massive force. I yelled loudly and horribly. The pain was extreme.

I lay quietly after it stopped. Silent and unmoving…

"Is he still alive, or is he dead?" Rx-100 asked.

"I'm fine with either," Vector snarled coldly.

I limply open my eye.

"Oh, get up, you weakling!" Vector screamed. "Now, for the last time, do you have accomplices, and if you do, where are they?!!!"

"I… I don't have accomplices. I came here alone," I muttered.

There were roars of laughter all over the room. Rx-100 displayed the word "LOL" on its screen.

"Foolish boy." Vector laughed. "You may have the pleasure of watching the world civilization disintegrate. Continent by continent will fall into the hands of me and my animal army!!"

"Please, can you tell me how you do it?" I pleaded.

"Very well," he said. "Firstly, I put collars on every animal as I have agents all over the world…"

"Tell him how you make the collars," George snarled.

"Oh, yes! I melt plastic bottles and add them to my machine, which converts them into the metal with the GPS and other things. Anyways…"

"But that increases climate change!" I exclaimed.

"Thought you'd care about that fake myth," Vector snarled.

"But it's very much real! You're putting the world in jeopardy!"

"Do I care? No! Now, listen if you don't want to be electrocuted again!"

I shut up.

"Next, I transmit a radio signal, only heard by animals to hypnotize them to do my bidding. I've done some tests, and they work. The collar leads them right here, and the animals are then stored in the storage room. They become more aggressive and fit to become my soldiers. They are programmed not to hurt anyone within the Vector society. Then with this animal army, I shall take over… the world!!!!! Any questions?"

I raised my hand.

"Great," he said and completely ignored me.

"Could you at least tell me about my mum?" I asked quickly. Then her name finally popped in my head for the first time in so long. "Her name is… Labake! Yes, Labake!"

"Aah, Labake," he said, nodding. "Yes, I know her."

"Really?" I asked, surprised.

"Yeah, she was a witch; they're hard to forget."

"What?!" I said, dumbstruck.

"Yeah, addicted to the wildlife she was. Wolves, deer, yadi, yadi, yada. I annihilated her eventually."

"What?!!!!" I said even louder.

"Mm-hm. It was a revolution. Everyone thought your mother was a curse to Arzeth. So, being the nice person I am, I neutralised her for them."

"You monster, you vile, wicked man! You knew it wasn't her; you knew it was a coincidence!" I screamed, my eyes stinging with tears.

"Yeah, I did, but I had to earn the village trust to let their guard down so I can rule the world," he said, grinning.

George laughed, but Rx-100 looked appalled at what Vector had said and turned around so as not to show it.

My ears were burning; I was furious.

Suddenly, I heard an alarm, loud and clear, then a man with a vector suit and neatly combed hair (with the comb still in it) appeared. His face was panic-stricken and filled with anxiety.

"The animals in storage," he said. "They've escaped and are trashing everywhere!"

"I suppose we'll chat later," Vector said to me. Then he left me and Rx-100 alone in the room.

"I am sorry about your parent," Rx-100 said. "I do not like Vector either."

"It's fine," I said, wiping my eyes.

Suddenly something popped out of the vent. It was Calvin and Aliyah!

"Hello, Ying," Aliyah said. "We're here to rescue you!"

Chapter Nineteen

The Reunion

"Calvin, Aliyah!" I exclaim. "I'm so glad to see you!" I felt a great rush of relief. The kind you get if you pass a very important test by just one mark. The kind of relief when you're falling straight into a volcano, but at the last moment, you realise it was only a dream. Needless to say, I was beyond relieved.

"We're here now; no need to worry," Aliyah said.

"I wasn't worried," I protested furiously.

"Ok," she said, sounding unconvinced. "Now, how do we get you down?"

"It's the button by that porcelain whale statue," I said.

Calvin went over and pressed it to get me free.

I felt as if a giant weight was taken off me. I stretched my arms and legs and scratched my body.

"Thank goodness," I yawned.

"Hurry up, *jarae*," Aliyah fumed.

"What's wrong with her?" I asked Calvin.

"Her dog passed away this evening. We found out just before we came looking for you," Calvin replied.

"I wonder…" I say. "How did you get here? How did you know where I was and…"

"Pardon me," Rx-100 speaks up. We had forgotten he was there.

"Stay back," I say.

"Wow!" Aliyah exclaimed. "That robot is adorable!"

"Thank you. It is a shame you have to be reported and e… e… eliminated." Rx-100 snarled.

"You don't have to," Aliyah pleaded. "You can do what you want to do."

"You are… are wrong. I shall forever be Vector's faithful servant."

With that, Rx-100's hand turned into a laser and pointed at us.

"Are you sure? Has he treated you well?" Aliyah asked.

Rx-100 paused. "N-not really that much," Rx-100 replied.

"Exactly. Do what you want, and don't let anyone boss you around. Just do the right thing," Aliyah responded.

Rx-100 stayed silent.

"Do what God wants," I said.

"What is God?" Rx-100 asked.

"God is almighty. The creator of everything in this world," I say.

Rx-100 stops aiming its laser. "I shall join God. He is my true master. Not Vecto… Vector. I shall join your side. God's side."

Aliyah squealed in excitement and hugged Rx-100 tightly.

Calvin spoke up. "Ok, so I'll tell you how we saved you from Vector's clutches."

"You know about Vector?" I asked.

"Yeah, I listened in the vents while Aliyah hacked the storage to let the animals out."

I was impressed. "Wow. Impressive," I said to them.

"Thank you," Aliyah grinned. "You know, I…"

"DO YOU WANT TO HEAR THE STORY OR NOT?!!" Calvin screamed.

"Ok. Calm down," I said.

He breaths in and out steadily. "Ok then. So I overheard you talking to yourself again last night…"

Aliyah gave me a questioning look. I ignored it.

"… Then I heard you go out, and I was about to follow you, but then I decided to call Aliyah, and we followed you together. It's like your reasoning transferred to my head and mine to yours…"

"Haha," I laughed sarcastically.

"... We saw you take on those guards; it was amazing! We took the tall one's clothes, and we stood on top of each other inside the uniform so that it looked like I was the feet and she was the head because she was good at talking and I'm good with leg movement."

"Clever," I remarked.

"We followed you around the vector company and figured out it was an ambush, but we couldn't tell you for obvious reasons, so we took the vents to sneak around," Aliyah said. "Somehow, Calvin found the animal storage, so I hacked it to cause a diversion so we can get to you, while Calvin watched over you, literally. When I finished, I came, and that's how we're here."

"Wow," I gasp. "You guys are amazing!"

"We're going to take them all down with our superpowers, though. Mine should be coming soon," Calvin said, smiling.

"Calvin. There are no superpowers," I admitted. "I made it all up."

Calvin paused.

"I... I knew," he said finally.

"Really?" I asked, unconvinced.

"Y-yeah," he replied. But I could see he was trying to hide his disappointment.

"Well, maybe you'll get bitten by a radioactive spider or something."

"I doubt it," Calvin sulked.

"Come on, Calvin, cheer up. You don't need powers or gadgets to be super. You've been a valuable member of this team, and because of that, both you and Aliyah have been promoted to the highest rank."

Aliyah nodded in agreement.

Calvin cheered up. "Oh, thanks!"

"We'll be the downfall of this vile Vector! At the count of three, all shout Super Power Club! 1, 2, 3."

"SUPER POWER CLUB!!!!!"

Chapter Twenty

Battle Plot

If we're going to do this, we need a well-organised plan," Aliyah announced.

"Agreed," Rx-100 says. "We need to find a safe place."

We all agreed. Lord Vector could come at any moment. We needed to maintain full vigilance at all times.

"Where could we go?" Calvin asked.

"I have a suggestion," Rx-100 beeped.

With a buzz, a loading screen appeared on his screen. It started loading from 1%.

"Won't take long," Rx-100 beeped jollily.

"Ok," I mumbled. I was in deep thought about what I was going to do. We're going to hold a mini-meeting in where Rx-100 is taking us, a brief one because we don't have time.

"Done!" Rx-100 dinged.

Then, at the side of Calvin, the floor opened up with a hiss. When the steam from below had cleared, we saw a descending staircase. I could hear a diminutive growl in the darkness.

"Come on," Rx-100 said.

We all took a big gulp with nerves. Aliyah went first, followed closely by Calvin, then I went last into the tenebrous chamber.

Going deeper below, it got darker and darker until I couldn't see anything anymore.

"We're here!" Rx-100 piped up in the dark. "Calvin, flip the switch beside you."

"How do you know there's a switch and where I am?" Calvin asked.

"Infrared vision is turned on," Rx-100 said. "Now flip the switch."

Calvin did, and the room was feebly illuminated by a single bleak bulb. It flickered a lot and affected my eyes.

I noticed we were surrounded by bags of rice, wheat and bags of meat.

"These are… are the foods for the animals," Rx-100 said.

"Why are you stammering?" Calvin asked.

"Oh, it's just a tiny bug, no big d-deal," Rx-100 said.

We weren't convinced.

"Ok, let's start a mini-meeting quickly," I announced.

"Af-affirmative," Rx-100 says. "Any ideas?"

"I've got one," Calvin said. "We-"

"No time for jokes, Calvin," I said. "Aliyah, do you have an idea?"

"Well, we could sneak through the vents and surprise them, beat them all up and just waltz to the radio signal and stop it."

"We do not all have the kind of combat ski-skills you might possess," Rx-100 said.

"I do," I confirmed.

"Besides, if we-we even get to the radio sig-signal, how do we stop it?" Rx-100 asked. "There isn't a switch."

"Well, I…" said Calvin.

"Shh, not now," I interrupted. "I think I…"

"STOP!!!!" Calvin shouted. "Let me speak!"

Calvin sighed as everyone was quiet. "I have 13 pieces of dynamite and 80 miniature bombs in my bag…"

At that point, I noticed he had a Minecraft bag with him.

"… We can use them to blow up the radio signal along with this company once we get out. Don't ask how I got them."

"That's… really good, Calvin!" Aliyah said.

"I agree," Rx-100 replied.

"You're on fire today," I exclaimed.

"Ok," Calvin says, taking charge. "We'll plant bombs on every floor while Aliyah guides the animals. Good?"

We nod.

"Ok, let's get going!"

But before we could set off, we heard a low growl somewhere in the room. Calvin became his normal, frightened self again and hid behind Aliyah. The noise grew closer and closer until something popped out from between the rice and wheat...

Chapter Twenty-One

The Plan Takes Place

Everyone went into a stiff silence and stayed still. And out came a snout, a little pink one that furiously sniffed the air around it. This showed it wasn't anything bigger than a bat. What if it was a bat? But bats don't have that type of nose. That's a relief. What if it was another badger? Oh no. These thoughts buzzed around me, and I kept my guard up.

Suddenly it jumped at Aliyah.

Calvin and I screeched while Aliyah gasped as she became engulfed in licks by the animal. It was a mouse. Its tail flicked about happily, and its white skin glistened under the dim light. It stared at Aliyah with friendly, red eyes.

Aliyah starts giggling. "It tickles," she said, laughing.

"Wow," Calvin gasped. "Why does it have those red eyes? I hope it's not controlled by Vector as well!" he exclaimed.

"It is common for al-albino animals to have red eyes due to lack of pigments in their ir-ir-iris *Buzz*" Rx-100 beeped.

"Wow!" Calvin exclaimed, gazing at it. He tried to touch it, but the mouse backed away and squeaked.

"It says it only wants me," Aliyah said. "But I'll try and convince it to let you pet it." Aliyah talked in chitters, and finally, the mouse nodded.

"Do it gently," Aliyah said.

"Yes… yes-yes Cal-Calvin is very care-care-carefullll… battery critically lo-low," Rx-00 said.

"Are you feeling ok, Rx-100?" I ask as Calvin continues stroking the mouse.

"I don-don't want t-to interfere with the mission, but no, I'm not ok; I haven't been charged in months."

Rx-100 did not look ok at all.

"You poor thing," Aliyah remarked.

"Where is your charging station?" I asked

"Last… floor… in… third… room… left. Shutting do-do-downnn," Rx-100 said, and its screen went black.

"Ok. How about we start downstairs and plant bombs on every floor from there upwards while Aliyah helps the animals, and on the last floor, we charge Rx-100?" I suggested.

We all agreed, and Rx-100 said he won't be hurt if he wasn't charged now, so we got to work.

* * *

Forty-five minutes later, we were in an elevator. The whole gang was here. Aliyah had successfully evacuated the animals without being seen, and Calvin and I had put bombs on every floor but the top one, which we were going to now. Aliyah had discovered a lot about her friend, the mouse, and their friendship had become stronger. She even named it Nibbles. It turns out it was one of the animals Vector had captured, but it broke its collar so it wouldn't be hypnotized.

When we finally got to the highest floor, we were jubilant. The last floor. This is where we needed to plant our final bombs to ensure this entire company would be destroyed. But first, we had to charge our little friend Rx-100.

We went into the room that Rx-1000 described. The halls were empty, which was just as well because we didn't need obstacles right now. Rx-100 was burning up and getting too hot to carry, so we really needed to hurry.

We finally got into the room and saw another tiny room, lit by a sad little light bulb, with a bed cover on the floor and a Tech Tribulations poster on the wall. It was the only joyful thing in the room.

"What is this place?" I asked.

"My… my ro-ro-room," Rx-100 replied weakly.

Needless to say, we felt very sorry for Rx-100.

"The charging station," Calvin pointed out.

Besides the blanket was a round object on the floor. I quickly put Rx-100 in it.

We waited and worried in silence…

And in five seconds, Rx-100 shot through the air, performing loop-the-loops.

"It's good to be charged again!" Rx-100 beeped.

"Great!" I said. "Now, let's go."

"Wait!" Rx-100 exclaimed. He then extended a hand from inside his belly, grabbed the Tech Tribulations poster, and stored it inside himself. "I just need that before you blow this place up. It is my favourite robotic band."

I wasn't convinced that existed.

I smiled, and I decided to place the last bomb for the floors until the radio signal right inside the bedroom.

"Is that ok, Rx-100?" I asked.

"Oh, it's fine. I hate that place anyways."

We left the room, and standing before us was Vector!

"Where do you think you're going?" he snarled.

Nibbles then squeaked and chomped hard on his hand. He screamed.

"Run!" I screamed.

Aliyah picked Nibbles off Vector's finger, and we skedaddled. As we reached the elevator, we heard Vector shouting orders. I tapped the button to the next highest floor after this. This is where I presumed the radio signal would be.

We went up before Vector could get us. I laughed nervously, but everyone else stayed silent.

After a while, the elevator juddered to a halt, and the door opened. I thought the radio signal would maybe be a size of an elephant. I was wrong; it was the size of a blue whale.

Chapter Twenty-Two

The Downfall of Vector Inc.

"It's massive!" Calvin called out. "I've got 52 bombs left."

With that, he took out sticks of dynamite and time bombs with matches. We had only used the time bombs, so we chose when to detonate them on Calvin's watch. He had a bomb detonating app, and I had no idea how it worked.

However, for this, we were going to use dynamite as well because after Calvin lights them, we would be out of there.

"After we've planted the bombs, we jump out the window," Calvin said.

"What?!" Aliyah exclaimed.

"That's very illogical, Calvin," Rx-100 said.

I look out of the window. "We won't survive a fall like that," I said.

"Well, heroes make sacrifices," Calvin said.

"That's suicide," Aliyah said matter-of-factly.

"Well, not exactly," Calvin replied. "It's for a good cause."

"Ok," I said. "So, we either get blown to smithereens or fall to our deaths."

"Let's jump. There's a little chance we may survive," said Calvin.

"The same with being blown up," Aliyah said.

"Jump!"

"Blown up!"

"Jump!"

"Blown up!"

"Jump!!"

"Blown up!!"

"Or fall into the clutches of a devious, devilishly handsome, terribly cunning, incredibly intelligent man such as myself!" cried Vector as he burst out of the elevator with George and two bulky men by his side.

"Vector!" I snarled.

"We meet again," he said. "And I see Rx-100 has… betrayed me." He growled menacingly and stared at Rx-100 intensely.

Rx-100 hid behind me. "Leave him alone," I said.

"It's genderless, you know," Vector said.

"Well, calling Rx-100 an "it" seems offensive. It has feelings. It's not a thing."

"Insolent child," Vector gnarled. "Jonathan, get them!"

The balder bodyguard approached us, cracking his knuckles menacingly.

We backed away precariously. Then suddenly, I felt a rapid surge of energy. I was pumped up and ready to fight. I stood on my toes and started jumping, staying in a combat stance and preparing to launch a blow.

I let out a battle cry. "Awooooooh!" I screamed and lunged at him. I pounded him more and more, not giving him a chance to hit me. I kicked, I jumped onto his head and started slamming it. Then I let go and head-butted him in his stomach. He toppled over.

Everyone stood in awe, except Vector. While I took heavy breaths, I let my guard down, and out of nowhere, a hand grabbed me by my neck and lifted me in the air. Jonathan had got up again.

I struggled furiously and desperately swung to and fro in an abrasive manner. "Let… me… go!" I cried out.

"Squeeze him!" Vector demanded.

Jonathan squeezed my neck profusely. I struggled harder, coughing and spluttering. This might be the end for me.

I was lacking breath, and my friends were screaming desperately for him to stop.

Suddenly, I felt a tingling sensation in me. I felt limp, my eyes were blurry, and I felt an aura around me. Everyone went quiet; I couldn't see as I was closing my eyes. It was like I was sleeping.

I opened my eyes to see that I was right. An aura was around me. A viridescent figure of a grey wolf was circling me. And I was holding Jonathan in the air with telepathy. I smiled. How did this even happen? I asked myself.

I felt like I was being hugged by my mum. The first one. This was the best comfort I've ever felt. With that,

I threw Jonathan aside with my newfound telepathy. He fell with a thud and stayed there.

"Uh… get him, Phillip!" cried Vector, panicking.

I simply grabbed Phillip and threw him aside with one hand. I had super strength as well!!

Vector gasped slightly and backed away. "You… you…"

"Calvin, throw the bombs at the radio signal!" I shouted.

He nodded and threw the time bombs, but with the dynamite, I used telepathy to set them all on fire. Calvin threw those as well all around the radio signal.

"Jump!" I scream. "And when we do, Calvin, detonates the bombs!

Aliyah put Nibbles in her pocket and cradled it; Rx-100 wouldn't die because he could float in the air, and Calvin was ready.

"3… 2… 1… go!" I screamed as we ran into the window, breaking it and falling. "Now!" I shout to Calvin.

He touches his watch screen and…

BOOOOMMMMMMMM!!!!!!!!

I smile that we defeated Vector before it went black…

Chapter Twenty-Three

The Vision

I WOKE UP IN A BLANK, empty room surrounded by nothingness.

I was a good child, so this must be what heaven was like. I imagined it to be less vacant and have a lot of fun things around as I interpreted from the Bible.

It was peaceful, though. I then realised I now had nothing to care about anymore, no responsibilities, nothing. I would just sit there for eternity until someone joined me.

I might as well start getting used to this. I lay on the floor and stared into the open space, wondering about my friends, family, unsolved businesses that I had left behind. This made me realise that despite having no responsibilities, this isn't as good as I thought it would be. I liked to learn and grow, and I hadn't finished. I never

even mastered algebra and long division. My heart fell. This wasn't paradise; it was a nightmare!

"Let me out!" I screamed. "Please let me out!" I ran around, screaming. "Help! Help me!!!" I waved my hands profusely, and tears stung my eyes.

Then I heard a loud bang sound behind me. I turned back and saw an ivory figure standing there. The figure sparkled and shone, and mist engulfed it.

"Are you… Jesus?" I asked uncertainly.

The mist cleared, and I saw… my mum! The original one.

"Mum!" I cried and hugged her. She felt soft and cosy, a familiar experience.

"Yes, it's me, honey!" she said with tears in her eyes. Her voice was soft and comforting.

"I missed you," I cried.

"I know you're a bit puzzled about a few things, some involving wolves, and I'll tell you the whole story," she said.

We wiped our eyes.

"So…" she began. "It all started in the fifth town I moved in as all the others kicked me out because I was apparently a witch."

"No…" I say in disbelief.

"Yes," she replied. "Because I… *we* come from a magical tribe that once thrived in the forest on an island south of the detached area of Arzeth. But we were all destroyed by invaders. We were the last surviving ones, and I swam into Arzeth with you on my back the whole time. However, I performed a little bit of magic that didn't hurt anyone, and someone saw, and this whole witch nonsense started."

I listen attentively.

"Before this, I had spent a good two months in Arzeth and had married your so-called daddy, Vector."

At this, my heart nearly skipped a beat, and I went pale. Vector was my father!

"Yes, the same Vector that tried to use an army of animals to take over the world. But don't worry, as you know, I had you before I married him, so you're not technically related to him. Your first father was the most hard-working, selfless man in the world. We wouldn't have survived if not for his… sacrifice." She choked, and a single tear trickled down her face that I wiped away.

At least I wasn't related to Vector technically. "But how come I never remembered him? I remembered you."

"I wiped any memory of him after what he did… I married Vector as he seemed a nice man at first, but… he betrayed me and turned the town against me. HE saw my magic; HE made them think I was a curse to Arzeth, He transformed me… into an angel."

I gasped. "What about all the wolf business?" I asked, trying to change the subject.

"Well, when I perished, I used some magic to turn into a wolf because it was my spirit animal and guide you again, but alas…"

I nodded sadly. She was that wolf, the one that raised me.

"What about that time the badger almost got me in that forest? Was that you that got me to safety?"

She nodded. "God gave me the power to, as performing that kind of magic is really difficult."

"Oh! And another thing, what is my name? My real name?"

She chuckled. "It's Jagunmolu."

When she said it, the ground shook a bit. I was surprised. I don't seem like that name, but I nodded anyway.

"Jagunmolu, my dear son, my spirit resides in you; you are filled with incredible power. Use it wisely, always be good, you're better than evil, and remember, I'll always be with you…"

With that, she faded.

"No!" I cried. "Don't leave me! Please!"

Then I woke up on something springy and cushion. I stood upright; I was on a trampoline—a large one.

"Ying! You're awake!" Aliyah cried out.

Calvin, Aliyah and Rx-100 rushed towards me.

I saw two grey wolves in front of me, and I was startled and backed away cautiously.

"Don't worry; these two wolves put a trampoline on the spot we were going to land and saved us. I don't know why, but we're alive, and that's all that matters!" Calvin exclaimed, gesturing to the two grey wolves. "They're friendly and won't harm us!"

I smiled and nodded, which was all I could do after such an experience. All I knew was that everything was clearer now.

Part 4

The End

Chapter Twenty-Four

The Final Battle

I GAZED AT THE FORMERLY great organisation, now in pieces. “We’ve done it, guys!” I announced.

We all cheered.

I petted the wolves, and they licked me affectionately.

“Aliyah tried to talk to them, but they were stubborn towards her and said they only liked you,” Calvin said.

“That’s because I have the spirit of the wolf,” I said, grinning proudly.

The others look at me, puzzled.

“Let’s go home, and then we can talk about it”.

As we made our way home, I heard something under the pile of rubble. I looked back, and I saw Vector coming out from underneath the glass and rocks.

The wolves growled, and so did I. The others turned

around, and upon seeing Vector, their eyes turned wide with surprise.

"Vector!" Aliyah cried.

"The one… and only," he panted. "Nothing stops Vector."

I had to admit, I was impressed. He managed to survive! George, Jonathan, and Phillip didn't, but I think the other of Vector's accomplices fled. They were still out there. The animals were safe too, but how could Vector take us on alone?

He brought out an ornate laser gun with a mix of lime from his pocket. "Take this!" he cried and shot it at me. A swift shot came out of the laser and pierced me right in my left breast, leaving a dark-green splotch with smoke rising from it.

I fell to the ground, clutching my chest copiously and clenching my teeth, trying not to shout.

"Ying?" Calvin said.

I rose. My face was in an ugly scowl, and my eyes were emerald and eerie. A dark red aura surrounded me.

"Jagunmolu, my son! You are under my control, and I demand you dispose of them!" Vector exclaimed.

"Son?!" Calvin and Aliyah exclaim, puzzled.

I howled and leapt onto Calvin, pinning him to the ground.

"Ying! I mean, Jagunmolu, please stop!" Calvin pleaded.

"All… hail… Vector!!!" I screamed and tried to bite Calvin, but Rx-100 pushed me off.

I landed with a thud but got up with ease. "You just made a huge mistake," I snarled, facing Rx-100.

"Sorry, Ying, but this isn't you," Rx-100 replied.

The wolves whined and nodded in agreement.

"I agree, Ying," Aliyah says. "Please fight it."

I got closer, my aura enlarging.

"You're not a villain…" She said desperately. Nibbles squeaked in agreement from inside her pocket. "… You're

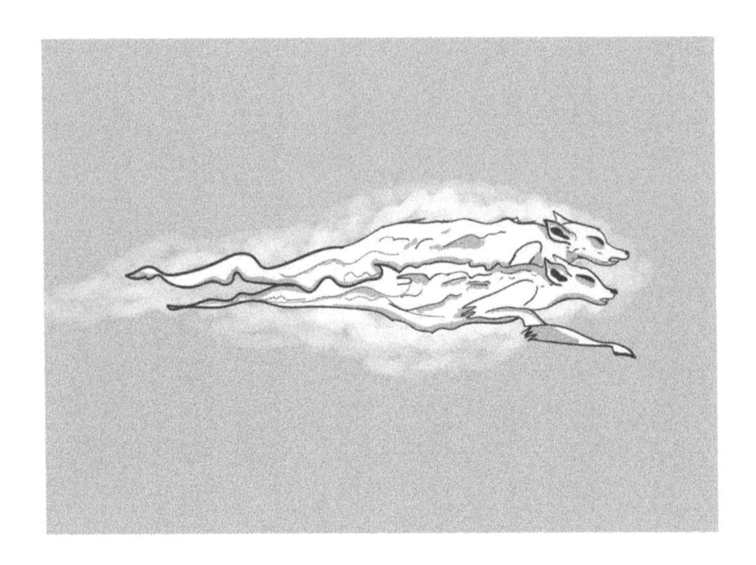

not a bad person; you're better than this. The real Ying doesn't give up, and neither should you!"

I got even closer, my aura burning, and suddenly… mum's words flashed in my head.

"I'm better than evil…" I mutter. "I… AM… I AM BETTER THAN… EVIL!!!!!" I screamed and released the negative red aura from my body, and the good one was revitalised.

I faced a flabbergasted Vector and released a massive shockwave, the same shape as a wolf—yet another reminder that my mum is always with me…

Then I saw, in the shockwave, another blue wolf combined with it.

... And my dad.

The powerful shockwave knocked the hypnotizing laser away from Vector's hand with massive force, and it shattered on the ground. Vector fell on the ground and was knocked out.

"Wolves," I say. "I present to you your well-deserved dinner," I pointed at Vector.

They licked their lips and carried Vector in their jaws all the way to the woods.

I laughed weakly and fell to the ground...

Chapter Twenty-Five

Happily Ever After

I GROGGILY OPENED MY eyes and saw Calvin's big, brown, curious eyes looking at me. Upon opening my eyes, he gasped.

"He's awake!" he cried.

"Enough jokes, Calvin," Aliyah says worriedly. "I'll call a doctor soon."

"No, I'm serious this time!" Calvin insisted.

"That's what you said fifteen minutes ago!" Rx-100 beeped.

"But..."

"Stop, Calvin; I'm warning you," Aliyah warned.

I was laying on Calvin's crisp-covered bed, I could tell. It was uncomfortable, so I stood up.

"Ying!" Aliyah gasped and hugged me, putting Nibbles down on the table.

"Good news, Ying/Jagunmolu," Rx-100 said. "After you fainted and we took you home, we called the police and reported the whole of Vector's scheme. Most of his accomplices are in jail, and as for Vector, well… you did say the wolves could eat him, so…"

I nodded, understanding.

"Well, the wolves would've taken him anyways, so it's not entirely your doing," Calvin said.

"Plus, the animals are now in zoos, and we get three free trips there each!" Aliyah added.

"Do our parents know?" I asked.

"Yeah. They just didn't know you were unconscious for over nine hours. We somehow managed to hide you from your parents for that long!" Aliyah said. "Also, my mum is fine with my Nibbles as my pet!"

"And Rx-100 as something we bought from China to our parents," Calvin adds. "Mum said she wasn't surprised with all this modern technology. But you still have to tell us about the wolf business and all that."

"I'll tell you after breakfast; I'm starving!"

And together, my friends and I destroyed the evil empire of Vector. I am Wolf Boy!

And Wolf Boy and the Super Power Club gang lived happily ever after!

The End

About the Author

ADEBOLA ERIFEOLUWA OLORUNSOLA is a 12-year-old boy with aspirations to become a famous writer, sharing the adventures of various fictional characters and their exploits. This is his first published book set in his hometown, Nigeria. He lives with his parents and two sisters in England. His creative mind is always thinking of new stories to share with the world. He has been writing from a very young age of seven. He is intensely fascinated by the art of literature and how to bring his imaginations to life in writing. He is a big fan of animals and mythical powers, which reflects in his writings.

Lightning Source UK Ltd.
Milton Keynes UK
UKHW011237080722
405575UK00003B/896